Stay Home

M Rubio

Copyright © 2020 by M Rubio

Stay Home

Sun outside

Life outside

By phone, she heard those supposed to be an advice words.

No option.

Again.

Same words had been already heard a long time ago, but now she was completely alone.

She could hear her heart beating, as during those awful days.

Dad was a civil engineer and Mom a lawyer.

She was 10 years old when the family moved to Colombia.

Dad had been invited to work for a multinational company in order to reconstruct Airport runway.

The project itself was based on the Olaya Herrera Airport runway reconstruction to its 2,508 meters in length by 45 meters in width and provide it with a parallel auxiliary taxiway, interconnected with the main one by nine taxing; seven of them high speed.

Other studies had already been started determining the necessity to build four international airports in Bogota, Cali, Barranquilla and also in Medellín.

Probably the family would stay there during a long time.

Their life in Medellin, at first, had meant a cultural shock, but despite the isolation of the rest of society, it was a really happy life.

Own school, club, friends.

Dad was ever working, then Mom was completely responsible by Daniela and her 12 years old brother, Paco.

They used to visit together beautiful and bucolic places, nature flooding their souls with tranquility.

However, this paradise, this wonderful place, was quickly transformed, generating constant fear in its inhabitants.

The guerrilla organizations, graved by the eruption and expansion of the drug trafficking problem, were directly affecting families lives.

Anyway, despite the news about it, families still had the feeling that the guerrillas were far away, that they were remaining hidden in the jungle, that life could go on.

Until that day.

They entered the city completely armed, looking for new members.

Their purpose was young people, who would be forced to fight for their cause, or die.

Poor families had been directly affected, as the fragility of houses had facilitated the entrance and young people kidnap.

Some parents were being shot when trying to defend their children, preventing them from being kidnapped.

Daniela, Paco and Mom had just arrived, from a walk, when they heard:

"Stay Home!"

It was a desperate voice and was coming from a group running around, trying to get to their homes and defend themselves from the guerrilla members, right behind them.

The three ran into the house, very perplexed, not yet understanding what was happening.

In the confusion, a shot was heard.

Quickly doors and windows had been locked by Mom.

They held each other for almost an hour, waiting for the guerrillas to get far enough away, for the danger to pass.

Mom was praying out loud.

Fear was hiding Paco and Daniela from speaking.

When the danger seemed to be gone, Mom screamed.

A desperate cry.

There was a lot of blood on her clothes.

For a few seconds it wasn't clear where that blood was coming from, until she realized that Paco had been shot.

Without wasting time or thinking about what was going on outside, Mom carried Paco into the car and the three of them went, as fast as they could to the San Vicente Hospital.

On the way, young and old people could be seen, fallen down, shot to death.

Around them the family, in despair, crying endlessly.

Others, looking at the infinite, an empty look, crying, trying to find the dear children who didn't know where had been taken and who would probably never find again.

They certainly tried to stay with Dad and Mom, to

"stay home".

The Hospital

Pain and Hope

She was feeling a lot of pain in her body and had high hopes to be seen by a doctor, medicated, cared for by nurses, since at home she was completely alone.

She also had a headache, but no fever.

Yes, she was feeling pain when urinating.

She tried to explain all her symptoms, hoping to be told which hospital to go to for treatment.

But when she mentioned her age, she received the information that looked like a condemn.

She couldn't go to the Medical Center nor to any hospital.

She had read about the ban on people over 65 from going to hospitals.

That at that age, that is, the people most vulnerable to the pandemic wouldn't be hospitalized.

She thought it should be a fake.

She had already experienced many extreme situations, during her life, including in war zones, and she had never known medical care to be limited to people due to their age.

The world had decided to establish a new "old age" because modern world life expectancy had been increased.

Along with life expectancy, the life quality has also been increased for them, so it should be no reason for people over 65 to be punished by prohibiting their admission to a hospital, just because their age.

Sure, it was a fake.

Not even that day, in a country without so many economic possibilities, had that happened.

She remembered path to the hospital to seem endless.

Mom praying and crying non stop.

Until they finally arrived.

The confusion at the hospital entrance was immense.

There was a crowd trying to get in, people hurt, others following their loved ones who were bleeding, looking for help, looking for care.

Some just were trying to find their beloved children, in the hope that they hadn't been kidnapped, that they had only been injured and would be there, being cared for.

Many nurses were at the entrance, trying to organize the crowd, organizing care in order of severity.

Pain, compassion and fear were stamped on their faces.

The wounded and their families were explaining their situation as if they were talking to an angel.

More than a situation explanation, it was seeming like a prayer.

Parents praying, children in despair, asking God for help.

Talking to the nurses.

Mom carrying Paco and asking Daniela not to leave her, to remain together, to grab her, not to get lost in the crowd.

A few minutes that felt like hours have passed on and mom was talking to a nurse.

Indeed, little was said, since the nurse understood the severity of the injuries and made them come in urgently.

Round of applause

clapping for everyone

deserved by some

not by other one

Every day she had been hearing the applause.

At first she tried to understand the reason for those applause, so she listened carefully to the news.

They were speaking of the sacrifices made by doctors and nurses, being in the front line of the battle.

What first line were they talking about?

So weren't them professionals who had freely chosen their activity?

As far as she knew, "in the first line", just doctors and nurses deployed to war zones could be considered, those deserving applause.

Throughout her life she had tried to develop an objective analysis.

She was always convinced that her actions and choices had to be aimed at achieving the best, both for her personal life and for humanity.

Sometimes she used to stop and wonder if she was being cocksure believing that her actions could influence humanity in general, but those moments she used to remember that a beach is made up of tiny grains of sand, each of them important for the cosmos purpose of creation.

She used to believe that each human being had the possibility, more than that, had the obligation to make a difference.

It wasn't necessary to be one of the geniuses of technology, of science, just to be a good human being, dedicated to own family, to own friends, to own job, already meant "making a difference".

Kindness, humanity, the search for perfection in the execution of your work is not supposed to waste time waiting for applause.

Of course, some jobs are generally considered to be more human than others, such as that of doctors and nurses.

This is because these professionals end up having a direct contact with human pain, also with contagious diseases, thus having, in theory, greater chances of becoming infected.

However, if we consider that they are the professionals with more knowledge of how to defend themselves against these diseases, how to protect themselves, we will see that there are others who, in reality, can be considered the true heroes in this area.

She had always considered that the real heroes were the ones who worked in cleaning hospitals.

These ones, without the necessary knowledge to their own defense.

So, the truth is that it's not a question of sanctifying a profession in itself, but the way in which each one proceeds when executing it, which must be valued.

She believed that a doctor work has a direct connection with the spiritual, since in many moments they "save lives", however, it is very important that they are aware that they aren't "God".

Let them be aware that their knowledge was allowed by the tireless work of human beings, who had dedicated their lives to studies and that such knowledge had been allowed by a superior being, that they aren't that superior being.

When she broke the femur, she had to endure that unbearable pain during 6 days, and to hear from doctors that they had, by law, up to 30 days, to surgery.

Thirty days by law?

It was simply cruel to say that she might have to endure that pain for so long.

She was hospitalized, she was medicated, but that pain was constant, even medicated.

How was the pain from 1 to 10?

"20"

She wasn't in a war, she wasn't in a without resources country, she was in a very well-equipped hospital, with many doctors and nurses, with an excellent structure.

So, why did she have to be waiting for the surgery?

This Pandemic had shown her the answer.

Doctors had the choice and people older than 65 should await younger ones to be seen.

That was the law.

A law making doctors to think being God, that they could choose who they should attend to first, based on administrative texts.

That the elders didn't deserve early care.

A cruel law, existing only to cover the difficulties created by incompetent politics.

A cruel law, whose cruelty those doctors didn't recognize by their own lack of empathy.

Certainly, in that huge hospital, with so many doctors, some should be more concerned with using their resources and knowledge to reduce the patients' pain, regardless of their age, but she wasn't lucky enough to be attended by one of them.

So, now, why should she go out to the counter and applaud doctors and nurses?

Which doctors should she applaud?

Those who were more concerned with meeting administrative regulations than understanding that her pain was unbearable?

Should she applaud the nurse who told her not to scream in pain because she was bothering her roommate?

Should she applaud the doctors and nurses who, instead of being interested in demanding resources and trying medicines that could be used since the disease beginning, ultimately saving lives, were colluding with politicians resolution that people should stay home even if being sick?

After all, doctors and nurses could be infected by doing their job, better patients not to be admitted to hospitals.

That didn't happen that day, in a country with far fewer resources, in a much less equipped hospital, with those nurses who looked more like angels, dedicated to reducing the others pain.

As soon as they got in, the impression they had was of a total chaos, but they could see that, in reality, everyone was looking for the sick and wounded people to be treated with the utmost urgency.

Paco had been immediately taken to an operating room.

Mom and she couldn't get in.

The next five hours had been impressive, without information, waiting for the surgery result.

The movement was constant.

Family members waiting, some receiving good news, others affected by a cruel reality.

The doctors hadn't been able to save their relatives.

Meanwhile, Mom was praying non-stop.

At one point, as if by magic, everything seemed to calm down.

Wounded people stopped arriving.

Doctors and nurses no longer ran down the halls, they were already walking normally.

Fatigue was evident on their faces, but they continued to behave with the same empathy when giving information to family members.

Mom just praying.

Loneliness

You can't be

You can not stay

You can't keep up

You can only pray

The news showing that those who had managed to be hospitalized were totally isolated from their families.

For sure, it was a Pandemic!

Everyone saying something about it and everyone wanting to be right.

"Everyone will be sick, whole humanity will be infected".

"No medicine has been yet confirmed effective for this disease."

"If no medicine is scientifically proven effective, we better not to use any medicine".

"We better prevent people from leaving home and being contaminated, or contaminating others."

She was thinking that if humanity had historically been content to simply hide, not to use the possible remedies because they weren't scientifically proven, we would already have gone back to the caves, or even worse.

Of course, some measures should be taken to prevent, as much as possible, people from becoming contaminated.

For sure, little was known about the virus, but surely the prohibitions imposed on the population impact, could be even more harmful than the virus itself.

Body's defenses were fundamental to face the possible virus effects, and the defenses are strengthened by the sun, by exercises, by tranquility.

Stress, sadness, can greatly weaken defenses.

So why are they condemning people to solitude, being them sick or not?

She knew very well the effect of loneliness on human souls.

Including loneliness felt being you accompanied.

That day, Mom was at her side, there were many doctors and nurses in the hospital, many family members of the injured people remaining, but she was feeling herself completely alone.

She was anxiously waiting for Dad to arrive at any moment.

When the doctor arrived, their souls were filled in with hope.

They wanted to hear how the surgery had been successful, how after five hour surgery the bullet had been successfully removed, the bleeding had been stopped and he would be in a room, waiting for their visit.

However, that doctor's gaze struck them like a sword of fire, reaching their souls.

With each word, despair took hold of that mother and sister.

They had done what they could, but the bullet had hit an important vein, it wasn't possible to save him.

She looked around and saw other mothers, other sisters in despair.

Where was dad?

She searched for words that could lessen her mother's despair, but her heart was also broken, in pain, she didn't know what to say.

That immense solitude, an immense emptiness, took over her soul.

She didn't know how long had passed on.

Mom had to take a tranquilizer and she stayed by her side, hoping she was ready to go home.

They would have to bring documentation to allow Paco's body to be removed.

She wondered if Paco would feel the same emptiness, the same loneliness that she and Mom were feeling.

She wondered if he would feel anything.

Where was dad?

Driving home seemed endless.

People could no longer be seen on the streets.

Where would they be?

The immense void was only broken by that woman, kneeling, weeping, screaming for God.

Dad would probably be home by now, desperate, not knowing where his family was.

Upon arriving, she ran in.

She wanted to talk to Dad, tell him what had happened, tell him about her sadness and how Mom was needing help.

They would no longer be alone.

But Dad wasn't there.

Where was Dad?

Mom came in next and sat down in the living room.

She stayed there for a long time, looking lost, as if looking at an invisible horizon.

She sat next to her and hugged her, hoping that this hug could lessen that pain they both were feeling, that intolerable loneliness.

She didn't know how much time had passed on when the doorbell rang.

Mom remained impassive, as if she hadn't heard and she went running, to open the door.

Probably Dad would have forgotten the keys in the office.

Yes, it would be Dad.

They would no longer be alone.

She was surprised to see Mr. Zamora, daddy's friend, asking for mom.

She knew Mr. Zamora, but he was very different.

His face was the embodiment of despair.

He was trying to smile and looking calm while asking Mom, but she saw on his face same despair of the woman who, kneeling, was crying and screaming for God.

Perhaps someone in his family had also been shot.

Maybe his son Andre had been also shot to dead.

But, where was Dad?

Mr. Zamora came in and talked to Mom.

Tears were wetting his face as he spoke, explaining that a bomb had hit dad's car.

He was trying to get home, trying to get to his dear family, to protect them from that desperate situation.

But Dad couldn't arrive.

He would never more arrive.

Loneliness was insufferable.

Mr. Zamora went on to explain that the company would take care of all the bureaucratic procedures for the family's return home.

Mom continued staring at that imaginary horizon.

Mr. Zamora said that all expenses would be borne by the Company.

That they weren't alone.

So, why that despairing loneliness in her soul?

My Refuge and
My Fortress

my God, in whom I trust

She used to watch every day news on TV showing the number of deaths rising each day.

Impossible not to think how this was possible, since the population was confined to their homes.

"Stay home" was the only action taken.

The World economy would certainly be very much affected, but without a doubt in her country it would be catastrophic.

Very few companies continued to operate, all of them linked exclusively to food or health.

The number of unemployed people was rising astronomically.

Small companies couldn't stand the situation and simply closed.

Streets totally empty.

People didn't dare to leave home due to fear and fines, except individually, to buy the food they would consume.

She thought how long people would have the resources to feed themselves and their families.

She was sure that many families would be starving, isolated at home.

So why did the number of infected people go up?

Were they lying?

Were the politicians using the situation, exercising a power of control that was giving them the feeling of being important?

Why did people just accept it?

Why was accepted that, once again, banks were the first to be supported by resources, instead of directing these resources to health, to hospitals?

She knew that the population can be manipulated by politicians and was sure that fear can be a great facilitator of such manipulation.

But she had never imagined that something like this was possible.

It was astonishing.

The death statistics going up every day, and the population was becoming nothing more than a statistic.

Perhaps in the future, when history books can describe the mistakes that were made by those who today exercise power, humanity can be informed of how many lives have been unnecessarily taken.

Maybe the answer would have been to treat infected people early in the infection, rather than keeping them isolated until little or nothing else could be done.

She was following news reporting some drugs that, when used at first, were supposed to help the body's defenses and were saving lives.

However, political discussions about these drugs were preventing their use.

The death toll was continuing rising.

Family members couldn't follow the funerals, only cemetery workers.

No matter what the religion was, no matter the pain generated in a family that couldn't say goodbye to loved ones.

She became surprised when she heard of a cemetery worker who, imbued with kindness and humanity, started to do, whenever the family would want, a life web connection in which the family could accompany the funeral.

She was delighted with this show of respect and humanity.

She hoped that in future history books there would also be deeds like this, which undoubtedly demonstrated that there are still

human beings concerned with the others
pain, without making politics, making the
difference.

Just like Mr. Zamora.

The company, in fact, took care of all
the expenses generated by returning to
Spain. Not only of them both, but also of the
transfer of Dad and Paco bodies.

They returned on the same flight as
the Zamora family.

They had also decided to return home.

Insecurity had become unbearable in
the country and fear was taking over all
families, especially those with young
children, the guerrillas and the drug
trafficking main objective.

Mom continued with her gaze lost on
the horizon, on that imaginary horizon, that
only she could see.

She hadn't spoken since she heard
about Dad.

Mr. Zamora took care of all bureaucratic details for their departure.

Grandma had been also contacted by him.

He arranged for her to be at the airport to receive them and for the bodies to be taken directly to the funeral.

A funeral had been organized by company representatives.

Mr. Zamora was greatly trying to lessen the pain, the suffering caused by such a tragedy to that family.

At the funeral were all Daddy's friends, Mama's friends, Paco's friends, in short, practically all the small town residents, in addition to Zamora family and company representatives.

All of them praying, asking God for those souls He was receiving.

Sadness could be felt in the air.

The sky, stained with dark clouds.

Mom was still lost on her own horizon.

School

Routine

Knowledge

Friendship

Fearless

Sadness

On TV and on overall internet sites, every day, many "experts" in every way.

Everyone giving advice, everybody wanting to be right.

Children couldn't go to school, as they had to stay home.

They would be with their parents, or with their grandparents, or with anyone.

Important was just to stay home.

Children would have internet classes, an hour or two a week.

They would receive the exercises to print, and to be corrected through the same route.

Group classes had been organized, once or twice a week, to fill in classes absence.

She used to think of this solution, imposed by politicians, and to ask herself:

Would that be a solution for all children?

Did all children have a computer available?

She knew that each family of medium economic situation should have at least one computer at home, which could be used for this purpose, but what about the printer?

What about the internet connection to support such classes?

What about poor families?

Right at the beginning of the ban on children going to school, it was discussed about children who depended on schools for their food.

How would they eat?

A food company proposed to send food to every needy child and she thought it had been a commendable humanitarian action.

However, a policy was opposed, saying it wouldn't be well-balanced food.

What?

Better to go hungry than to eat unbalanced food?

As if by magic, nobody was talking about it anymore.

What about the children who were depending on the school for food?

As emerged from the depths of hell, countless experts appeared, talking about psychology and the influence of the situation on children.

She used to listen to the comments and started to think that 80% of those people, those experts, shouldn't have contact with children, didn't know the real influence that that situation was causing them.

All of them discussing the absence of classes, the harm it could cause to the children, as if this were the only trauma that was being caused.

She believed in the importance, for example, of children's contact with their grandparents, the good that their hugs have always done to souls.

No hug from grandparents.

Covid-19 was loose.

She also believed in the need to play with friends, now that wasn't possible.

Covid-19 was loose.

They couldn't go out to sunbathe, that sun that their parents always said to be necessary.

Covid-19 was loose.

Covid-19 was bad.

But what is Covid-19?

What monster would children have to face if they went to school, if they went out on the street, if they met with their friends, if they hugged their grandparents?

It must surely be a super monster, since not even adults could explain very well what it is.

Adults only say that you have to be afraid of Covid-19.

And they fear the super monster, even without knowing its appearance.

She was watching children's reactions, always on the windows, and realized that fear had taken over.

Children no longer wanted to leave home.

Possible fines were limiting parents, but fear was preventing children from leaving home.

Fear of the invisible monster had affected an entire generation.

The world would have to learn how to help children overcome such stress.

Grandma wasn't an expert in any field, had no university and wasn't a psychologist.

She had survived a civil war and could understand the war's effects on souls.

This knowledge was fundamental so that Daniela could overcome fear impregnated in her being.

She had an incredible strength, which endured a kindness and delicacy when dealing with Mom and Daniela's pain.

This fortress was a pillar on which Daniela was leaning and her kindness and delicacy were a balm for her soul.

Mom had never recovered herself.

Doctors had talked about a stage of schizophrenia caused by a deep depression.

She would always remain watching her personal horizon, without communicating, wrapped in her own thoughts.

They said that in this state, her pain was more bearable.

Grandma never failed to take care of Mom, but her main concern was to insert in Daniela the necessary strength to overcome this situation, to bring normality to her life, a routine of overcoming.

Normality.

Grandma's economic situation wasn't the best, she had to keep working to be able to meet the expenses for maintenance of the three of them.

She managed to find a Day Center that would take care of Mom so that she could work and that Daniela could study.

She used to say that routine and normality were fundamental to her development.

That fear Daniela was feeling during the first year of her return, had been controlled.

Leaving home was causing her, in the early days, an extreme fear.

She couldn't leave home without Grandma to hold her hand.

First days at school were desperate.

She was feeling as if an invisible monster could destroy her at any moment.

But all of that had been overcome with Grandma's strength, guidance and love.

Daniela, now, would wake up early every day to help Grandma prepare Mom to go to the Day Center, also to get herself ready for school and for the three of them leave home.

Mom in the Center, Grandma on the way to work and Daniela to school.

These used to be the best hours of Daniela's day.

She had made friends, being very popular.

She was very curious about the World History, it was her favorite subject.

She was especially interested in Colombia's history, having an inner need to understand what had happened, what historical reasons would have influenced her family's life so dramatically.

But Grandma ever told her not to make it an obsession.

She tried to.

Grandma was right.

Routine and normality installed at home made happiness invade their lives.

Mom situation was already part of their life, without generating sadness.

It was normal.

Her normalcy.

When Grandma died, a new blow to her life was felt, with such crudity, that she thought she couldn't recover.

But the teachings of those years, friends always for her, helped her to overcome all that sadness.

She looked for her new routine, her new normality.

Daniela has been already a teacher and needed to look for the best way to take care of her mother, lost in her own horizon.

It was impossible to take care of her alone, so she chose to have her admitted to a Center, where she could have all the care, including the medical one, she needed so badly.

Her friends tried to stand by her as much as they could, in order to help her overcome all that sadness, but the loneliness that had been settled in her home, was looking invincible.

Each time she was arriving home, she had to make a great effort to enter.

However, the weight of sadness made her just to want to stay home.

She was no longer wanting to leave, except to go to work.

Solitude had taken over her soul.

It was when the Zamora family visited her that everything changed.

He was a little changed, he looked like his age and years of hard work, but he still had that kind look.

Mr. Zamora had brought her a gift.

Her name was Hope.

A two-month-old Pitbull, whose eyes captivated her.

Hope immediately threw himself into her arms, playfully, stroking her as if he knew she needed him.

Mr. Zamora, once again, had shown his sensitivity and the affection he felt for Daniela.

Hope would be the balm that would remove any sign of loneliness from that home.

Now she was ever wanting to go home to take care of her new friend.

Hope used to accompany her on her outings with friends.

Whenever she had to leave alone, she used to tell him to behave, that she would be back soon, that he should stay home.

Her new routine, her new normality.

No fear.

No loneliness.

Hope

New normality

Everybody talking about the new normality.

Everyone giving their own opinion about what is happening in the world, about the changes that will happen in human beings, due to Covid-19.

Daniela's feeling was that the world was looking like chaos.

With every call she was making to the urgencies number, she was feeling that there was anything but emergency care.

People were forbidden to go directly to doctors and hospitals.

They should first call to see a doctor over the phone.

Being seen by a doctor over the phone?

How was that possible?

Every time she got someone to answer, on the other end of the phone, she was absolutely sure that wasn't a doctor.

Of course, they were using words that tried to demonstrate their medical knowledge, but Daniela wasn't convinced.

It looked more like a trained team, like the ones hired by law firms to charge the borrowers.

They were very well trained.

More than once she heard that they were professionals.

Professionals?

She had heard such statement more than once and couldn't help thinking that if someone wants to identify himself, he says:

"I'm a doctor"

"I'm a nurse"

"I'm a surgeon"

But when someone says:

"I'm a professional"

the statement becomes very vague, somewhat forced, one can almost doubt to be truth.

When she started to feel that exaggerated fatigue, she tried to receiving the needed guidance by calling.

But, in all the callings, she made, just had felt that finding a way to get her to take some medicine that could make her at least feel better, wasn't those people objective.

Their only goal was to prepare a spreadsheet with her data, making her more a statistical number.

She didn't quite understand why no medicine could be taken.

She knew it was a new virus, an unknown variable of a known virus.

An unknown variable of a known virus?

So it was known or unknown?

If people aren't left in their homes without medical advice if they have a simple cold, without indicating that they strengthen the body with vitamin C, why they were now ordered to stay at home without the slightest indication.

It was a variation of a known virus, which was attacking the body's defenses.

So why did the doctors not prescribe drugs that could strengthen these defenses?

If the sun and exercise strengthen the body's defenses, why were people confined to their homes?

WHO, in the beginning had made some statements, risked guesses about the virus and the disease and how it would affect each and every human being.

Until they began to contradict themselves.

One day a drug wasn't suitable, the next day it could be, but there was no scientific evidence to support its prescription.

Of course!

It was an unknown virus, or rather, an unknown variable of a known virus, it hadn't yet been treated.

So was it better to let people get worse enough to no longer have the slightest solution?

People started to die alone at home.

Was it better to allow them to die in that inhuman and immoral way, than to try to use the drugs that could possibly save their lives?

WHO did not want to be blamed for actions that were taken, so no action was their solution.

This was the worst technicians team that WHO had ever had.

In countries where doctors weren't so involved with politics, where their actions weren't so controlled by politicians, patients began to be treated with these drugs, not approved by WHO experts, but which were already approved drugs during more than 70 years.

Of course, treatment was important to be given right at the contamination beginning, so the person's organism wouldn't be so weakened and could react.

Thus, in many countries, the contamination curve was being, now, accompanied by another curve:

People were heated when early medicated.

But not in her country.

Social Security was in government hands, doctors worried about not losing their job, blindly obeying the guidelines, however absurd or inhuman they might be.

She stopped looking for guidance over the phone, as she came to the conclusion that no solution could be received through this route.

Hope's company was essential for her to feel better, it was like an angel accompanying and caring for her.

She was continuing following the news on TV and was informed of the chaos created by the opening and closing of borders.

She always thought about why to confine people to their homes, generating so much unemployment, so many companies that had simply disappeared, if during such confinement the contamination had only increased.

If people didn't have contact with other people, how did they get infected?

Now there was more flexibility and the companies were back up and running, looking for a normality that, surely, would only be achieved in two or three years.

The financial losses had been enormous.

People had already instilled in their routine the cleaning of hands and clothes when in contact with other people.

Sanitize all packaging that arrived at purchase was part of this routine.

The use of masks was mandatory outside home.

When it all started, Daniela commented to friends that she thought it was incredible that the government could prevent the population from coming and going, a right that she believed to be constitutional.

Some friends told her that if people weren't obliged, they wouldn't be able to understand the situation and wouldn't do what was necessary, that is, they wouldn't increase hygiene, they wouldn't use masks.

She didn't believe that.

She believed in the human being and the ability to adapt.

She also believed that if there had been advertising from the beginning indicating what should be done, people would have the ability to adapt themselves and do what was necessary.

Of course, it was necessary to work on this orientation.

She certainly believed that the so-called "risk group", people over 60, should, whenever possible, respect a more careful isolation.

This should be proposed.

More difficult, but not impossible, would be to convince young people to defend themselves against that invisible monster.

Children had developed an incredible fear, now they had to be helped to overcome it.

However, young people, in general, in the history of mankind, have another way of facing this type of problem.

They generally deny it, so as not to feel vulnerable.

The fact that they had simply been prevented from leaving had given them a feeling that the ban had reasons other than medical.

A mental chaos that now had to be resolved.

Mom was still at the Senior Center.

Although there was an extreme concern with older people, with the deaths that had happened in such Centers, Daniela was following the news, trying to know the Centers situation and Mom's one wasn't part of the statistics.

Daniela was feeling better, that probably hadn't been Covid-19, probably would have been the result of the stress of the situation.

Anyway, she was feeling better.

She has high hopes that the situation would be resolved and she is confident that the human being adaptive power is immense.

For sure, some changes will occur, as normally happens, but only for those who want to do something better with their experiences.

Those who don't allow themselves to be just a manipulated object.

The ones who would also draw the best of any situation, not necessarily from chaos.

And for sure, belonging to the risk
group due to her age, whenever possible,

without obsession,

she will,

with Hope,

stay home

www.ingramcontent.com/pod-product-compliance
Lightning Source LLC
Chambersburg PA
CBHW061630130726
47996CB00003B/1216